11,95   10,76

Santa
Claus
around
the
world

LISL WEIL

HOLIDAY HOUSE / NEW YORK

1818

Library of Congress Cataloging-in-Publication Data

Weil, Lisl.
Santa Claus around the world.

Summary: Describes how people around the world
celebrate Santa's arrival.
1. Santa Claus—Juvenile literature. [1. Santa Claus]
I. Title.
GT4985.5.W45 1987   394.2′68282   87-45334
ISBN 0-8234-0665-2

No matter what shape or name he goes by, Santa Claus has
been a beloved visitor and gift-bringer at Christmastime for
as long as anyone can remember.

Everybody knows that he flies from the North Pole in a sleigh
pulled by reindeer, and slides down chimneys to deliver gifts.

But there are children
who no longer believe in
Santa.
They say, "There is no real Santa! It's only my dad in a red
suit, or some fat men standing around in stores."

One little girl, thinking it over, says, "Santa is a spirit. He is
loving and caring, and he is very old."

The truth is that the Santa we know is all these things. Hundreds of years ago, there really was a Santa. His name was Nicholas, and he lived in Asia Minor. He was a very kind and caring bishop who helped the needy and sick.

Sometimes his help came in wondrous ways. There are many stories about his good deeds.

Once, it is told, he kept an old, poor, and sick father from selling his daughters into slavery. He gave them enough gold nuggets to live in peace.

Another time he took to the air, flying quickly. He saved a ship and its sailors from a raging storm, a wild sea, and horrible sea monsters.

Nicholas also brought three boys back to life. They had been chopped to pieces and salted in barrels by a greedy, cruel butcher.

Nicholas was finally made a saint, because the Church believes that only a saint can perform such miracles.

Saint Nicholas's greatest love was for children, most of all good children. To make them happy, he always brought them extra-special treats.

Since then, children and grownups around the world have celebrated his coming every year. Although his most popular name today is Santa Claus, people in foreign places know him by many other names, too. Some countries even have female figures who bring gifts just as Santa does.

Each country has its own stories and ways of remembering its gift-bringers.

Saint Nicholas's holiday was first celebrated in Europe.

The children of the Netherlands called Saint Nicholas Sinter Claas, Sinter Claes, or Sint Nikolaas. Nowadays he is known as Sinterklaas. He does not fly from the North Pole. Instead, he arrives by ship on December 6. Then, riding a white horse, he puts his gifts into the wooden shoes of good children. In the olden days, children set out hay, carrots, and water for his horse. Bad children watched for Black Peter, who traveled with him. He had sharp horns and a big red tongue, and he waved sticks, threatening to carry off bad boys and girls in his huge sack.

When the Dutch settled in North America, they brought along this fine holiday. Although they stopped wearing wooden shoes, their custom of using them to hold Santa's gifts may have led to hanging stockings by the fireplace. In time, the Dutch name Sinter Claas changed to Santa Claus, and he became part of the American holiday season.

The children of England also loved this gift-bringing holy man. Way, way back they called him Father Christmas because he brought his gifts at Christmastime. Decked out in holly, he would arrive riding a white donkey or even a goat. Today he is sometimes called Santa Claus, too.

In parts of France, Santa is known as Petit Noël, which means "Little Christmas." But mostly he is Père Noël, which means "Father Christmas." Wearing a red suit and cap, he is loved by French children.

Some parents say he has a helper called Père Fourchette, or Father Fork, because of his long horns. Others say his helper is called Père Fouetard, or Father Whip. He twitches his whip at any child who has been naughty!

Though Switzerland is a small country, the Swiss have a mixture of languages and customs.

Boys in the German-speaking city of Zurich are especially lucky. They can become helpers to Samichlaus, as they call their Santa. They wear long white nightshirts, funny cardboard masks, and lit-up headgear that they make themselves. With their bells and trumpets making loud noises, they parade through the main street on Samichlaus evening.

The boys also help to distribute Samichlaus's gifts of cookies, fruits, and nuts to the young and old lining the sidewalks.

Up in the mountain villages, where the Swiss speak a quaint dialect called Romansh, folks have a gift-bringer called Christkindl (Christ Child). Though this angel has wings, he visits children riding a sleigh pulled by reindeer.

When Swiss families moved to America, they brought along their Christkindl celebration. In America the name Christkindl soon sounded like Kriss Kringle, which in time became another name for the Santa we know now.

Children in Germany have two gift-bringers. They
have a Christkindl who sometimes looks like a girl
angel and sometimes looks like the Christ Child. In
early times, the angel was often pictured next to a
white donkey.

Today, the Germans also have a Weihnachts-
mann, or Christmas Man. Christkindl and Wein-
achtsmann bring gifts on Christmas Eve.

People in Germany have always loved to sing. The Nürnberger Sternsinger were one of many early groups singing praise to Saint Niklaus and Christkindl.

Another old German holiday custom was for a little girl to dress up as Christkindl. With wings and a crown, she would hand out gifts to other children. It was an honor to be chosen, and the Germans talked about the custom even after they came to America. This is another way that the name Christkindl became Kriss Kringle and finally a different name for Santa himself.

The Germans are famous for making beautiful toys, and their Santa toys are sold all over the world.

Children in Austria and Hungary used to call Santa, Nicolo.
Today, he is better known as Niklaus. His sidekick, a furry
figure of a devil, is called Krampus. With his rattling chains
and big empty sacks, Krampus looks as if he could make
naughty children disappear!

December was an extra-busy time for Austrian candymakers. They made rows and rows of rounded figurines of Nicolo. Then they filled each of the hollow bodies with jelly beans and bonbons—candies with fruit-and-nut centers. During the twelve days before Christmas, parents bought these for good children. But there also was a Krampus made of juicy prunes. Even for a naughty child, it was a tasty treat!

In northern Italy, Saint Nicholas brings gifts on December 6. But Italian children also have another favorite gift-bringer, an old woman named Befana. An ancient legend tells how Befana claimed to be too busy to join the Three Wise Men in bringing gifts to the child in Bethlehem. To make up for her error, Befana now appears every January 6. With a bell to announce her arrival and a cane as a warning to naughty children, she slides down chimneys with gifts for good children.

We know that the early Russian children called their gift-bringer Miracle Man. Now he is called Grandfather Frost and arrives on New Year's Day.

In Russian folklore, there is also a gift-bringer named Baboushka. Like Befana, she was too busy to go find the child in Bethlehem. Since then, she searches for him in every house she visits, and leaves sweets and small gifts behind.

The children of Scandinavia have bearded Santas, just as we do. In Sweden they are called Tomten or Jultomten

and are quite small. They used to arrive on Christmas Eve in a sleigh pulled by a Julebock, a Christmas goat. Today their sleigh is more often pulled by reindeer.

In Denmark the Santas are even tinier and look like elves. They are known as Julenisson. Denmark also has a Christmas Man called Julemanten.

In Spanish-speaking countries, Saint Nicholas is only one of many saints and not a special gift-bringer.

But today in Mexico, a Santa figure is present when the children break their hanging piñatas (clay or papier-mâché jugs) with sticks to make the gifts inside spill out.

The gift-bringer in Japan is an old priest called Hoteio-sho who travels by foot. He is said to have eyes in the back of his head to see if children are behaving. He rewards good children with gifts out of his backpack.

In Korea, "Santa" wears a hat and carries his gifts in a wicker basket on his back.

Chinese children outside mainland China hang up their stockings for their gift-bringer to fill. He is called Dun-che-lao-ren.

Here in the United States, Saint Nicholas first looked like a bishop. He carried a staff and rode a white horse. One old picture shows him followed by Black Peter carrying a big box of Saint Nicholas's gifts.

However, as many more people from different countries moved to North America, Saint Nicholas began to look like England's Father Christmas and the Dutch Sinter Claas.

Today, all over the United States, Santa Claus arrives on Christmas Eve wearing a red suit and cap. Though many houses have no chimney for him to slide down, he always finds a way to get indoors.

Post offices open extra departments at Christmastime to handle the many letters that children write to Santa Claus.

So, wherever he is, Santa and his gifts fill a special place in the hearts of all children.

Because Santa is so beloved, he is celebrated in stories and poems, in songs and plays, in pictures and parades, on radio and television, and in films and shows.

Santa's likeness appears on gadgets, on greeting cards, and even on children's clothes. And there are toys of all sizes and shapes with his image.

When Dad wears a Santa outfit, he is like a Santa's helper, bringing joy with his gifts just as the real Saint Nicholas did in his time.

Store Santas are Santa's helpers too, collecting money for needy people.

In fact, everybody can become a Santa's helper by lending a helping hand. Even little ways of showing care can make a loving gift . . . and not on holidays only.

About Santa Claus

Saint Nicholas was born over 1,500 years ago in Asia Minor, now part of Turkey. He became a bishop at an early age. Then called "a boy bishop," he performed good deeds. It is said that he died about sixty-three years later, on December 6, about A.D. 343.

Clement Clark Moore, a professor at General Theological Seminary in New York, wrote a poem in 1822 called "A Visit from St. Nicholas." It appeared in the newspaper *Troy Sentinel* in 1823 and is popularly known today as "The Night Before Christmas."

Washington Irving, a nineteenth-century American writer, described Santa's appearance during a dream in his book *Diedrich Knickerbocker's History of New York.*

In time for Christmas 1873, the first issue of the *St. Nicholas Magazine* was published for children.

The American president Benjamin Harrison liked to dress up as Santa for his grandchildren.

In 1897, a famous letter written by eight-year-old Virginia O'Hanlon was printed in the New York newspaper *The Sun.* In the letter, Virginia asked if there really was a Santa Claus. The paper's editor, Francis P. Church, wrote this answer: "Yes, Virginia, there is a Santa Claus. He exists as certainly as love and generosity and devotion exists and you know that they abound and give to your life its highest beauty and joy."